A delightful picture book for young children that illustrates familiar everyday objects.

Encourage your child to talk about the objects, and ask simple questions such as ''What colour is this?'' and ''Where do we find this?'' The most important thing is to make looking at the book fun for both of you!

Each illustration contains something red (the red collar in the picture of the dog, for example). Point these out to your child as you look at the pictures together. Then ask him or her to find the red section in each picture.

The blue, yellow, and green picture books in this series may also be used in similar ways.

Acknowledgment:
The publishers would like to thank Maureen Hallahan for the hand lettering used in this book.

British Library Cataloguing in Publication Data
Baby's red picture book.
   1. English language. Words—Illustrations—
For children
I. Dillow, John
428.1′022′2
   ISBN 0-7214-1088-X

Published by Ladybird Books Ltd Loughborough Leicestershire UK
Ladybird Books Inc Auburn Maine 04210 USA

Printed in England

Baby's
RED
picture book

illustrated by JOHN DILLOW

Ladybird Books

house

tree

toothbrush

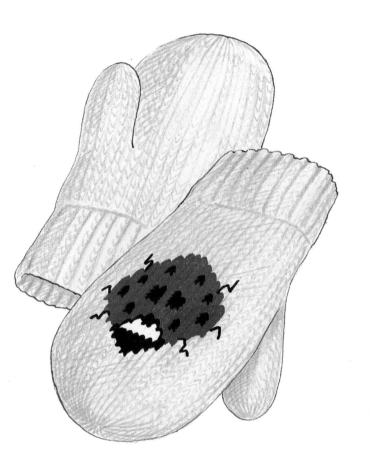

mittens

shoes

dog

teapot

pegs

cake

car

chair

cockerel

clown

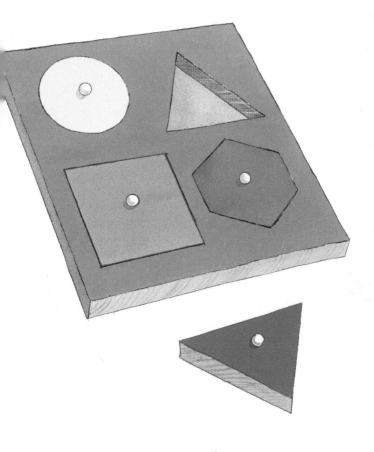

puzzle

apples

keys

sledge

tricycle

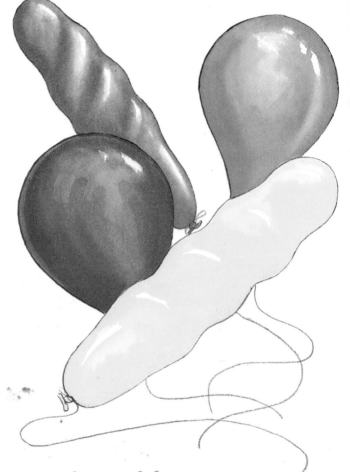

balloons

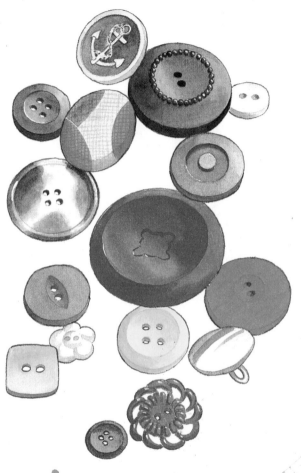

buttons

scissors

present

book

clock